KATHY HENDERSON has written many successful books for children. Her titles include *The Middle of the Night, A Year in the City, The Little Boat* – winner of the 1995 Kurt Maschler Award, shortlisted for the Smarties Prize and Highly Commended for the Kate Greenaway Award, and *The Storm*, which was shortlisted for the Kate Greenaway Award. Among her books for Frances Lincoln are *15 Ways to Go to Bed* (shortlisted for the Smarties Prize), *The Bedtime Book,* with Penny Ives, *Cars, Cars, Cars!,* illustrated by Charlotte Hard, and *Tabby Cat,* illustrated by Susan Winter. Kathy lives in North London.

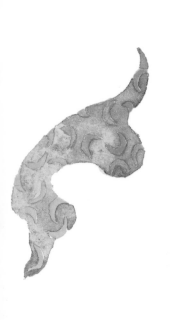

*for Charley, Daniel
and baby Annie who helped;
with a special thankyou
to Melody.*

15 ways

to get dressed

Kathy Henderson

FRANCES LINCOLN

15 ways to get dressed

"I'm going to dress like Batman,"
"I want to have blue hair."
"I have to look like my friend Lyn,"
"I don't care what I wear."

"I love putting my best clothes on."
"Wait! I've left my mac."
"My shorts don't fit."
"My jeans have split!"
"It itches down the back!"

"I've got to take my costume,"
"Who's put egg on my leotard?"
"Why should I wear school uniform?"
"D'you know where my gloves are?"

"I'll just put on my roller skates,"
"I won't go out unless
  I wear that hat."
"Stop, stop, cos that's
  fifteen ways to get dressed!"

Ten clean nappies

We've got a little baby,
she's very very small,
not long ago
she wasn't here at all,
but as soon as she was born
all naked and hot,
what was the very first thing
she got?

That's right,

nappies,
nappies,
nappies,
nappies,

ten clean nappies
in a box.

The first one she peed on
the second one she screamed on
the third one she kicked up over her head
the fourth one she was sick on
the fifth one wouldn't stick on
the sixth one leaked all down her leg
the seventh one tore
the eighth hit the floor
when we did up the ninth
it slid straight off again,
then she frowned,
and before
we could fetch any more
she did something smelly
in nappy number ten.

Sock hop

Where's my sock?

Dad, I can't find my sock!

Where is it?
I had it.
It's vanished.

Last night?
Well I dropped it
like I always do
and now there's just one
where there ought to be two.
Where's my sock?

What's it like?
It's like this one,
sort of green, sort of blue
and all thin at the back
where it's nearly worn through.

Yes of course I've looked …
Well … on the lampshade
and under the bath,
by the bookshelf,
in the rubbish bin,
I've done lots of looking
but I can't find my sock!

What?
No I haven't got another
and I want this one's brother.
I've already got a sock pile,
a stockpile of odd socks,
I'm fed up with lop socks
and lopsided hopsocks!

Oh!

Thanks Dad.
Where was it?
What, here on the chair?
Well who put it there?
er … Dad? …
Have you seen my shirt?

Clothes are daft

"Clothes are daft.
Why've I got to wear them?"
Gloria Corker always said
when she got up, "I mean it's mad!
Why stuff your toes in knitted bags,
hang saggy dragging raggy things
around your body, arms and legs
and fix them on with zips and strings
when you could wear nothing,
absolutely nothing,
when you're already wearing
beautiful
no-fuss
skin?"

Thumb-Twisters

Buttons and zippers and poppers and things,
buckles and velcro and laces and strings,
push them and pop them and tug them and tie them,
tangle your fingers and stumble your thumbs.

Hold up the towel

Hold up the towel Mum,
or somebody'll see me
changing into my swimming things,
oh cover me up please!

Hold the towel up properly Mum,
it's starting to slide
and I haven't got my knickers on
and everyone'll see my bum
and now I've got my foot stuck
oh help! My costume's all full of
sand inside.

Hold the towel tighter Mum,
it's flapping in and out.
I'm sure somebody's going to look
and I haven't got my top on yet.

Right. There we are.
You can let go now.
That's strange,
there isn't anyone about!

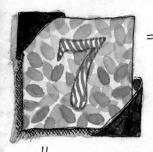

Twin Teaser

Ebenezer Teaser and his twin brother Tim
looked exactly like each other and always dressed the same,
but where Ebenezer Teaser was as neat as you please
his twin brother Tim was a terrible mess,
yes,
his twin brother Tim was a mess.

"How d'you look so neat?" said Tim to his twin.
"Well," said Ebenezer. "It's really quite easy.
I don't like wrinkles or creases or crinkles,
when I put on my clothes I pat them flat,
I fasten my buttons and I pull up my socks
and they just seem to stay like that,
there's nothing to it,
they just seem to stay like that.

"So why," said Ebenezer, "don't you do the same
if you want to look smart?" "Well I do," said Tim.
"But when I put my clothes on they always button up wrong
and I've scarcely turned round before my shirt's hanging out
and my trousers go baggy and my socks go saggy
and everything flaps about,
that's the problem,
everything flaps about."

"Well perhaps after all it isn't such a bad thing,"
said their mother to the brothers, "cos you're like as two pins
and if there wasn't this way to tell who is who
I don't know what the rest of us would do,
no, I can't imagine what we'd do."

Dan

Dan puts his pants on
over his ears,
puts his legs in his jersey
T-shirt under one armpit,
he doesn't mind a bit
about anything you say.
Who cares
if everyone stares?
Dan puts his clothes on his way.

Dan puts his knickers
on top of his head.
Both
feet
in one leg of his trousers
socks on his hands.
"I'm a dog," says Dan.

And then he takes his clothes off
from time to time too.
Like just after he's put them on
or when everyone else
is about to go out.

He pulls off his socks
like knitted spaghetti
        stretching and
                stretching
                        enormous
                                long
                                        toes.
                                Shorts come off
                        in a bundle
                        knickers go flying.

                        Now he's got an arm stuck

                Dan's in a tangle
        with the undershirt monster,
        red in the face, he looks half strangled
        but he doesn't want help
                "Get off! Let me do it!"
                        Dan can dress all by himself.

Who says?

"Girl babies are pink
and boy babies are blue"
and "you can't wear a dress,
you're a boy, it won't do"
and "you won't want hair ribbons
or bracelets or bows
or flowery patterns
or frills on your clothes."

But who says?

"Well you *can* wear pyjamas
and trousers and boots
as a girl, yes, and shorts,
yes, and superman suits.
But if you want to look pretty, dear,
–and of course you do –
you'll wear your best dress
and your black patent shoes."

Who says?

Why not dress like a duchess
or dress like a clown,
wear whatever you like
inside out, upside down
and just for a change
try breaking the rules
so that nobody else
but just you says,
that's who.

Dressing up

I've got a hat
and I feel fine,
ten miles tall.
Get off! It's mine.

I've got big shoes,
I'm a clown,
when I lift my arms
my pants fall down!

I've-got-a-box
I-am-a-mach-ine
an-au-to-ma-tic el-ec-tron-ic
sub-mar-ine.

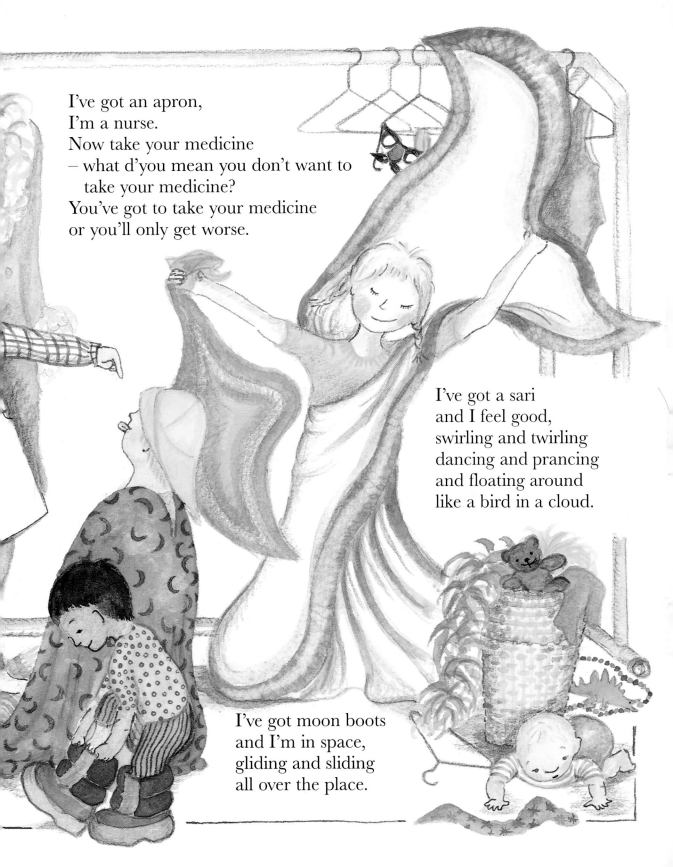

I've got an apron,
I'm a nurse.
Now take your medicine
– what d'you mean you don't want to
    take your medicine?
You've got to take your medicine
or you'll only get worse.

I've got a sari
and I feel good,
swirling and twirling
dancing and prancing
and floating around
like a bird in a cloud.

I've got moon boots
and I'm in space,
gliding and sliding
all over the place.

Growing

One morning when Tom Smith got up
he found his clothes were all too tight,
his arms and legs were sticking out,
he looked a most peculiar sight.

"I can't do up my trouser tops,
the bottoms just won't reach my feet,
my shirt's too small, the cuffs have burst,
can't move my arms, the sweater's worse.
I know they fitted yesterday!"

His brother laughed, "Come and see, Mum!"
"No. Tell him to put some others on,"
his mother called,
"and hurry up, it's half past eight,
you haven't had your breakfast yet,
it's school, you're going to be late."

Tom scrummaged through his cupboard, but
everything that he pulled out
was just the same:
too small, too tight, too short, too thin.
He squeezed them on then off again,
"Mum! Someone was at my clothes last night!"

Tom Smith, half dressed, was hopping mad.
"Right, who's been messing with my things?
And if you think I'm going to school
tied up with string and safety pins
you're wrong. Don't laugh! I'm not a fool!"

His brother stopped and wiped his eyes,
his mother said, "I'm not surprised
at all. I don't know why you moan,
they haven't shrunk, it's you that's grown!"

New shoes

I've got new shoes
straight from the shoe shop shoes.
They're still clean underneath.

These shoes are smooth shoes,
not a scratch or a scuff
or a dent or a bump,
they're blue shoes
with bright white stitches
and the size showing clear
on the clean insides.

My shoes smell sweet,
nobody's feet have ever been
inside them until my feet,
and they squeeze and they squeak
as I walk down the road
with a shine on the toes
of my new shoes.

I can't

I can't take my coat off
or I might die.
If you make me take my coat off
I'll cry and cry and cry.
I know it's very hot
and I've got a lot of clothes on
and everyone is staring
and none of them are wearing one
but I can't take my coat off
so please don't try.

Lizzie Liddle

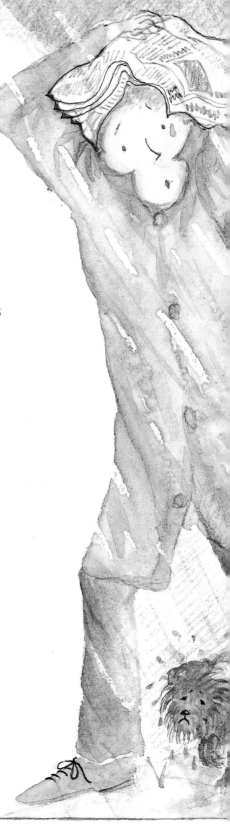

Lizzie Liddle didn't like it
    when the weather was wet.
She couldn't stand the feel of raindrops
    trickling down her neck and shoulders
or her wet skirt flapping round her legs
    each time she moved,
or dripping hair, cold hands and squidgy socks
    and squelching shoes.

So this time when the rain began
Lizzie hatched a brilliant plan.

She took
        not just wellie boots
        a coat with a hood
        splash suit trousers
        gloves and an umbrella,
        but two big broomsticks
        a plastic sheet
        and an old crash helmet
        she found in the cellar
        some nails and string
        4 carrier bags
        12 rubber bands
        and a few old rags
and
she made herself a suit with a walking roof.
"At last," said Lizzie, "I'm waterproof."

Lizzie Liddle
stepped out smiling
into the pouring rain,
but
she only got half way
down the street
before the sun
came out again.

Pyjamas

In the morning somebody puts their head round my door
and says, "Time to get up."
I am up. I've been up for hours.
What they mean is, it's time to come DOWN
and have breakfast.
So I do.

So then they say, "Aren't you dressed yet?"
I am dressed. I've got pyjamas on.
But they say, "Stop arguing and go and get dressed."
What they mean is, go and get UNdressed.
So I do.
I go up, take my pyjamas off,
and start again:
knickers, socks, shirt, sweatshirt, fiddle, fiddle.
Right. That should keep them happy.
But does it?
No.

They have that look. You know the one?
The your-collar's-bent-in-and-you've-got-odd-socks-on look.
The you-can't-wear-that-just-look-at-it look.
So I do.
It looks fine to me
and anyway it's time to go.
So what happens now?
That's right,
they say

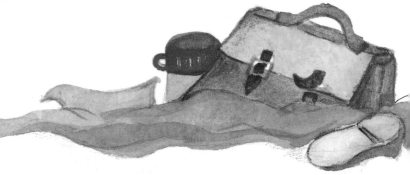

"Your shoes aren't done up, and don't forget your coat.
Of course you need a coat. It's not summer now you know."
So I put my coat on, even though I know
I'm just going to have to take it off again
at the other end.

In the evening it all happens again.
Backwards this time.
"What are you wearing your coat in the house for?
You'll roast!"
"Do you have to leave it on the kitchen table?"
and "If you're going to put your feet up on the sofa,
at least take your shoes off!"
Until in the end they get right back to the beginning,
"Go and put your pyjamas on. It's time for bed."
And always when I'm doing something really interesting,
"Pyjamas … Pyjamas … PYJAMAS!"

Wouldn't it be a lot simpler
If I just kept them on all day?

I don't care what you think I look like
I don't mind if you think I'm strange
I like wearing anything I feel like
You should try it for a change.

MORE PICTURE BOOKS BY KATHY HENDERSON FROM FRANCES LINCOLN

15 WAYS TO GO TO BED
Written and illustrated by Kathy Henderson

An exuberant and humorous collection of poems and pictures,
showing the many entanglements, games and surprises
surrounding the nightly pantomime of getting ready for bed.
This lively and original collection was shortlisted for the Smarties Prize.
ISBN 0-7112-0589-2

CARS, CARS, CARS!
Illustrated by Charlotte Hard

Welcome to the incredible world of Cars, Cars, Cars!
Zoom through the car factory and the showroom, past roads and roadbuilding,
to the garage and the scrapyard. Witty text and fizzing pictures
show the jams and pollution as well as the fun.
For car fanatics from 3 to 103.
ISBN 0-7112-1382-8

NEW BORN
Illustrated by Caroline Binch

Words of welcome from the family introduce a newborn baby
to his earliest sensations. Kathy Henderson's warm evocation,
and Caroline Binch's expressive artwork introduce brothers and sisters
to the excitement of a new baby, and will enchant
parents-to-be and grandparents alike.
ISBN 0-7112-1393-3

Frances Lincoln titles are available from all good bookshops.
You can also buy books and find out more about your favourite titles,
authors and illustrators at our website: **www.franceslincoln.com**